ANIMALS HAVE COUSINS TOO

ANIMALS HAVE COUSINS TOO

FIVE SURPRISING RELATIVES OF ANIMALS YOU KNOW

GERALDINE MARSHALL GUTFREUND

FRANKLIN WATTS
NEW YORK • LONDON • TORONTO • SYDNEY
A FIRST BOOK • 1990

The story about the hyrax's call is based on an account in B. Grzimek's
Grzimek's Animal Life Encyclopedia, vol. 12, Van Nostrand Reinhold
Company, 1972. The quote from the *Journal of Mammology* is from an
article by Kenneth G. Johnson, George B. Schaller, and Hu Jinchu,
"Comparative Behavior of Red and Giant Pandas in the Wolong Reserve,
China" in *Journal of Mammology*, vol. 69, no. 3 (1988), 552–564.

Cover photographs courtesy of:
Cincinnati Zoo (top) and Little Rock Zoo (bottom).

Photographs courtesy of:
Cincinnati Zoo and Botanical Garden: pp. 15, 17 top,
31, 35, 36, 52 top (all Ron Austing), 17 bottom, 19 (Mark Alexander),
25 bottom, 33, 35 both top, 39, 43 top, 45 top right, 46, 52 bottom;
Chicago Zoological Society: p. 21 (Mike Greer); Mike Dulaney: pp. 23,
25 top, 26, 41, 43 bottom, 45 bottom; Virginia Zoological Park: p. 29
(Laurie Wagoner); Columbus Zoo: p. 45 top left (Nancy Staley);
Little Rock Zoo: pp. 49, 51, 55, 56 (all Debbie Jackson).

Library of Congress Cataloging-in-Publication Data

Gutfreund, Geraldine Marshall.
    Animals have cousins too : five surprising relatives of animals
you know / Geraldine Marshall Gutfreund.
        p.   cm. — (A First book)
    Includes bibliographical references.
    Summary: An introduction to the principles of evolution and
taxonomy, illustrating how animals have developed and changed
over time.
    ISBN 0-531-10861-9
    1. Evolution—Juvenile literature.   [1. Evolution.   2. Animals.]
I. Title.   II. Series.
QH367.1.G87   1990
591.3'8—dc20   90-31027   CIP   AC

For my daughters:
Audrey, who loves to learn, and
Rachel, who loves pandas.

CONTENTS

Thanks to the Cincinnati Zoo, especially
Barbara Brady, Michael Dulaney, Herb
Kingsbury, Thane Maynard, Ed Maruska,
Lisa Moreschi, Beatrice Orendorff, Paul
Reinhart, and Steve Romo; to the Columbus
Zoo, especially Nancy Staley and Don
Winstel; to the Indianapolis Zoo, especially
Andrea Martin; to David Westbrook of the
Little Rock Zoo; to Peter Crowcroft of
Salisbury Zoological Park; to the Virginia
Zoological Park, especially Laurie Wagoner;
and to the World Wildlife Fund.
Also thanks to librarians Jackie Kohrman
and Eileen Mallory, as well as writers—
and good friends—Teresa Cleary, Linda
Kleinschmidt, and Jean Syed, for their advice
and for reading the manuscript; and
to my husband, Mark, for his support.

INTRODUCTION
WHOSE COUSIN IS WHO?

Animals have cousins too. You know what giraffes, elephants, giant pandas, rhinoceroses, and koalas are, but do you know their surprising cousins: okapis, hyraxes, red pandas, tapirs, and wombats?

Usually when you say that someone is your cousin, you mean that he or she is the child of your aunt or uncle. You both have a set of grandparents in common. This person is your first cousin. But a cousin can be someone more distantly related to you. You and a person who have the same great-great-great-great-great-grandparents are also cousins.

Individual animals have first cousins as you do, but when a scientist says that two kinds of animals, such as a wolf and a dog, are cousins, the scientist means that they are distant cousins. They *evolved*, or developed, from the same kinds of animal ancestors, or great-great-great-etc.-grandparents, perhaps millions of years ago.

Scientists study animals to see how closely they are related to one another. They study the *fossils*, or hardened remains, of the ancestors of modern animals. They study the body parts of modern animals to see if they evolved

Red panda—found in Nepal, Bhutan, Tibet, Burma, and southwestern China

Malayan tapir—found in Burma, Thailand, West Malaysia, and Sumatra

Wombat—found in Australia, including Tasmania and Flinders Island

GREENLAND

Barents Sea

ICELAND   NORWAY

DENMARK

NETHERLANDS

BELGIUM   FINLAND

UNITED   SWEDEN

KINGDOM   USSR

IRELAND   E.   POLAND   CZECHOSLOVAKIA

W. GER.   AUSTRIA

GER.   HUNGARY

FRANCE   ROM.

SWITZERLAND   YUG. BUL.   *Black Sea*

ITALY

PORTUGAL   SPAIN   GREECE   TURKEY

ALBANIA   SYRIA   IRAN

Caspian Sea

LEBANON   IRAQ

MOROCCO   TUNISIA   ISRAEL JORDAN

SAUDI   OMAN

WESTERN   ALGERIA   LIBYA   EGYPT   ARABIA

SAHARA   YEMEN

MAURITANIA   MALI   NIGER   CHAD   SUDAN   S. YEMEN

SENEGAL   UGANDA   ETHIOPIA

THE GAMBIA   BURKINA   CENTRAL

GUINEA BISSAU   NIGERIA   AFRICA   KENYA   SOMALIA

GUINEA   CAMEROON   RWANDA

SIERRA LEONE   GABON   ZAIRE   BURUNDI

LIBERIA   TANZANIA

IVORY COAST   CONGO   MALAWI

GHANA   ANGOLA   ZAMBIA   MADAGASCAR

TOGO   ZIMBABWE

BENIN   NAMIBIA   BOTSWANA

EQUATORIAL   MOZAMBIQUE

GUINEA   SOUTH   SWAZILAND

AFRICA

LESOTHO

CANADA

UNITED STATES

*ATLANTIC
OCEAN*

MEXICO

CUBA   JAMAICA

HAITI

BELIZE   DOMINICAN REP.

GUATEMALA   HONDURAS   GUYANA

EL SALVADOR   NICARAGUA   SURINAME

COSTA RICA   FRENCH

PANAMA   VENEZUELA   GUIANA

COLOMBIA

ECUADOR

ANDES MOUNTAINS   BRAZIL

PERU

BOLIVIA

PARAGUAY

*ATLANTIC
OCEAN*

CHILE   URUGUAY

ARGENTINA

Okapi—found in Zaire, mainly in the Ituri Forest

Hyrax—found in Africa, including Zaire (text explains
habitats of bush, rock, and tree hyraxes), and in the
Middle East (only rock hyraxes)

Other tapirs (South American, Baird's, woolly
tapirs)—found in Central and South America

from the same kind of ancestor. They study how animals' bodies work—how they move, digest their food, and reproduce their young. They compare how animals behave—how they get and eat their food, protect themselves, make their homes, mate, and care for their young—to see how alike they are. Most recently, scientists have been studying chemicals in animals' bodies. Animals that are similar in all of these ways may be cousins.

Then scientists *classify* the animals, or divide them into groups, depending upon how closely they are related. Three modern animals may have had the same kind of animal as evolutionary great-great-great-grandparents. This makes them all cousins. But if two of the animals also had the same kind of animal for great-great-grandparents, they are closer cousins.

Think about dogs, wolves, and foxes. Dogs are thought to have evolved from wolflike ancestors a long time ago. A wolf is a dog's close cousin. A longer time ago, foxes shared a common ancestor with both wolves and dogs. A fox also is a dog's cousin but not as close a cousin as a wolf.

It is easy to guess that dogs, wolves, and foxes are all cousins. They look similar, and they act similarly. Some animal cousins do not look or act alike. At least, it does not seem that they do, until they are closely studied. These cousins, because they live in different places, or *habitats*, or for other reasons, may look different. They may act differently. They may even look or act like an animal that they are not closely related to.

Now meet the giraffe's striped cousin, the okapi. Come explore.

CHAPTER ONE

OKAPI
THE FOREST GIRAFFE

Imagine that you are crouched in the dark Ituri Rain Forest, which is in the central African country Zaire.

You see glimmers of sunlight through the leaves. Or do you? The sunlight is ambling away on four long legs—both right legs together, then both left. You glimpse an animal that appears to have the legs of a zebra, the body of a small reddish-brown horse, and the head of a giraffe. The animal is eating leaves with a 14-inch (36-cm), blue-gray tongue. You have discovered the only living relative of the giraffe, the okapi.

Okapi means "donkey of the forest." In the late 1800s, the Mbuti pygmies, who live in the Ituri Forest, told English explorer and journalist Sir Henry Morton Stanley about an animal they hunted called an okapi.

Stanley later told another Englishman, Sir Harry Hamilton Johnston, about the okapi. Johnston had once read about a unicorn living in Equatorial Africa, and he thought that the okapi might be the fabled unicorn. He went to Africa in search of it.

Johnston found only sets of *cloven* hoofprints on the forest floor. He obtained from soldiers in Africa two belts made of the striped portion of okapi skin. Johnston mistakenly announced in 1900 that he had discovered a new *species* of zebra. In 1901 an officer sent Johnston two okapi skulls and a complete skin. After studying the skulls and the skin, the scientist knew that the okapi was not a zebra. The okapi is in the same family as the giraffe. The okapi can be called a forest giraffe.

A male okapi's horns (left) are less than half the height of a male giraffe's horns. Both male okapis and male giraffes use their horns to fight other males of their own kind, but they fight other enemies with their legs and hooves.

Scientists found that these animals are alike in two important ways. First, the okapi and the giraffe are the only *ungulates*, or hoofed animals, who have bony structures on their heads—horns or antlers—that are both skin-covered and permanent.

Deer have antlers that are covered in velvety skin, but deer shed their antlers and grow new ones. Cattle have permanent horns, but cattle horns are not covered in any type of skin. Only okapis and giraffes have horns that are both skin-covered and permanent. Usually, only male okapis have horns. Both male and female giraffes have horns.

The second way in which they are alike is that both okapis and giraffes have special *canine teeth*. These special teeth let okapis and giraffes quickly comb small twigs and leaves off trees and bushes.

Modern scientists have also found that chemicals in the blood of okapis and giraffes are very similar.

Since okapis live in rain forests, they look different from giraffes, who live on plains or in areas with only a few trees. The giraffe, who is 13 to 17 feet (3.9–5 m) tall and weighs 1,200 to 4,250 pounds (554–1,928 kg), would not be able to get around in a dense rain forest. The okapi, who is 5 to 6 feet (1.5–1.8 m) tall and weighs 465 to 550 pounds (210–250 kg), moves easily through the forest.

On the plains, the giraffe needs to see far to spot food and enemies. In the rain forest, it is more important to smell and hear well. The okapi does not see as well as the giraffe, but it smells and hears better.

The giraffe's brown spots help hide it from enemies in open areas of sun and shadows. The okapi's stripes look like sunbeams shining through dark leaves. They protect the okapi from human hunters and leopards. The okapi's stripes may also help an okapi calf keep its mother in sight.

Giraffes live in herds to protect themselves in open areas. Okapis can protect themselves better alone in the forest, and they form pairs only briefly to mate.

Asengu (the larger okapi) and her first mate,
Poko, at the Cincinnati Zoo. On December 12, 1989,
Asengu gave birth to a female calf.

A female okapi is pregnant for about 15 months. She gives birth to one calf. The calf is darker than its parents and has a short mane, which later disappears. After a year the calf leaves its mother. Okapis in zoos are known to live up to 25 years.

Okapis, like giraffes, are usually silent. But their calves bleat, and zookeepers have heard adult okapis cough and whistle. Asengu and Max, okapis at the Cincinnati Zoo, are described by one of their caretakers as making a "chuff-chuff" sound.

Okapi-like animals lived 15 million years ago, giving rise to modern giraffes and okapis. Some scientists think that the okapi is a living fossil. These scientists think that in a rain forest little disturbed by humans, the okapi has not needed to change much from its early ancestors.

Okapis once had a wider range but now are known to live only in Zaire, mainly in the Ituri Forest. If people begin to cut the forest trees and use the land for building, okapis could be lost forever in the wild. In case this ever happens, zoos are caring for and breeding okapis, creating an "animal bank." If their habitat were later restored, there would be okapis to return to the wild.

The World Wildlife Fund and the government of Zaire are making plans to preserve part of the Ituri Forest as the Okapi National Park. Such a park would allow okapis, other animals, and plants to live undisturbed.

CHAPTER TWO

HYRAX
LITTLE BROTHER OF
THE ELEPHANT

Now it is night in the forests of Africa. Sit around the camp fire and listen to the storyteller talking about the hyrax, another animal of the forest. Listen to the hyrax calling to find a mate or to claim its part of the forest.

"Hear," says the storyteller, "how Hyrax came by his strange call. Once, Hyrax was caught by his enemy, Leopard.

" 'Please,' begged the little Hyrax, 'let me eat some juicy leaves before you eat me.' He added slyly, 'They will make me even plumper and tastier.'

"In return for this favor Hyrax promised to call out to let Leopard know he was still near. Just as he does today, Hyrax first began to call softly, 'Drr-drr-drr.' Then he moved farther and farther from Leopard, but to make Leopard think he was still near, Hyrax called louder and louder. 'Ahua, ahua,' screamed Hyrax until he had climbed high into a tree where Leopard could not find him."

How the hyrax got his call is a story, but it does tell us some facts about hyraxes. The kind of hyrax found in the African forests, the tree hyrax, is *nocturnal*. Leopards are one of their main enemies (they are also preyed upon by eagles and African golden cats). They do make the sound in the story. Their screams may last for over five minutes and can be heard by other tree hyraxes up to a mile away. They live mostly in trees, though one type of tree hyrax is found living among rock boulders in Africa. They are small animals, weighing from 3.5 to 10 pounds (1.6—4.5 kg). They eat jungle plants, especially the leaves of jungle trees.

There are two other *species* of hyraxes. The largest, the rock hyrax, lives in rocky areas in the grassy plains, moun-

These rock hyraxes, also called dassies, keep warm
by huddling together, basking in the sun, and lazily
resting for long periods of time. An African story
tells that Dassie has no tail because he was too lazy
to travel to King Lion's court when Lion was
giving all of the animals their tails.

tains, and very dry areas of Africa. Rock hyraxes also live in rocky areas of the Middle East. They weigh between 4 and 12 pounds (1.8–5.4 kg).

Bush hyraxes are smaller, weighing between 3 and 5 pounds (1.4–2.3 kg). They are found in Africa, in mountains, forests, and grassy plains. Some kinds of bush hyraxes live in trees, but most live among rocks.

Rock hyraxes and bush hyraxes sometimes live side by side. This is very unusual, as often there is not enough food for any two species that are members of the same family of animals to live so closely together. Scientists think that bush hyraxes and rock hyraxes can live together because rock hyraxes eat mostly grasses, and bush hyraxes eat mostly leaves from bushes and trees.

Rock and bush hyraxes are active mostly during the day. As with tree hyraxes, leopards are also their enemies. Other enemies are eagles, lions, hyenas, and snakes. Bush and rock hyraxes whistle, scream, and chatter.

Just as the hyrax in the story fooled the leopard, real hyraxes fooled scientists for a long time about what animals they were related to.

Hyraxes look something like guinea pigs. Scientists first classified them as related to guinea pigs. They were given the family name Procaviidae. This means "before the guinea pigs." Later they were given the name hyrax, which means "shrew mouse."

Hyraxes are not closely related to guinea pigs. They are not closely related to mice.

These small animals are part of an unlikely group of cousins—including the elephant, who weighs 6,600 pounds

Both elephants and hyraxes sometimes use their long upper incisor teeth, or tusks, as weapons.

Aardvarks are African animals. They are sometimes called antbears and earth pigs, but they are
most closely related to elephants and hyraxes.

(2,294 kg) to 13,200 pounds (5,987 kg), more than the weight of four cars. This group of animal cousins includes elephants, hyraxes, and the sea mammals, manatees and dugongs. All of these animals are thought to have descended from a common ancestor and are known as *paen-ungulates*, "almost hoofed ones." Recently, because of chemical studies, some scientists also group aardvarks with these cousins.

How did scientists ever guess that the tiny hyrax is related to the giant elephant? Parts of their bodies are very much alike. Scientists compare the legs and feet of animals to see if they are related. The leg bones in hyraxes and elephants are very similar. Both hyraxes and elephants have flattened nails on their feet.

Hyraxes have rubbery pads that contain sweat glands on the bottoms of their feet. These pads help them grip surfaces like tree trunks and rocks and help them to climb.

Scientists also study teeth to see if animals are related. In elephants and hyraxes, the same teeth, the *incisors*, grow large. These teeth are the elephant's tusks. Male dugongs also have tusks. When a hyrax opens its mouth, you can see tiny tusks. Tusks in other mammals are usually formed by the canine teeth.

Scientists have studied the blood of hyraxes, elephants, manatees, and dugongs. These studies also show similarities.

Elephants and hyraxes also have similar wombs, where their young form. The nipples from which the young nurse are also in the same place on the mothers' bodies. Another clue to hyraxes' relationship to elephants is the long period that hyrax mothers are pregnant with their young.

Most small animals are pregnant for short periods of time—1 to 2 months. Hyraxes are pregnant from 7 to 8 months. The hyrax has a short pregnancy compared to the elephant's 22-month pregnancy but long enough to show scientists that hyraxes and elephants once had a common ancestor.

Hyraxes give birth to between one and four young. The babies nurse until up to 5 months old. Rock and bush hyraxes live together in groups called colonies. Tree hyraxes live alone, except when mating or nursing their young.

Fossils show that 40 million years ago there were hyraxes as large as bears. There were few other animals where they lived of their same size and competing with them for the same food. Thus, the hyraxes thrived. There were at least six kinds, in sizes varying from the size of modern hyraxes to the large hyraxes. Then, 25 million years ago, other animals, such as antelopes, moved into the same areas and ate the same food as the hyrax. Eventually, only small hyraxes survived. They survived because they lived among rocks and in trees where the antelope-type animals didn't go.

The ancestors of hyraxes and elephants survived in opposite ways. The hyraxes survived only in small forms, but the elephants survived by eventually evolving into very large animals. Large animals are able to eat less nutritious parts of plants. The large elephants were able to eat woody parts of trees and shrubs, which the antelopes and horses who shared their habitat could not eat.

A young rock hyrax is weighed at the Virginia
Zoological Park. At this zoo, four or five
rock hyraxes are born each spring.

Hyraxes are hunted for their fur, but their biggest danger is the destruction of their habitats. Most in danger are the tree hyraxes because many of the African forests are being destroyed. The same preservation of forest areas that will help the okapi will help the tree hyrax.

Hyraxes are found in zoos. They are known to live up to 12 years.

Before you leave the forest, listen to the hyrax, which African storytellers call "little brother of the elephant."

CHAPTER THREE

RED PANDA
CHILD OF THE MOUNTAINS

You are on the trails leading to the Himalayas, the mountains of Nepal, Bhutan, and Tibet, and on into the more ancient mountains of Burma and southwestern China. You are exploring high in these mountains, higher than 8,000 feet (2,438 m). The mountains are cool and misty, so cloudy that parts of them are called the cloud forest. Bamboo, the toughest grass in the world, grows here.

Look carefully in the trees. You see, camouflaged by reddish-brown moss, a red panda. The red panda is one of two animals called panda, which is a word from Nepal meaning "bamboo-eater."

In southwestern China you might also see the better-known giant panda. Giant pandas eat little except bamboo leaves and stems, though they will eat meat when it is given to them. Red pandas mainly eat bamboo leaves, but they also eat fruit, roots, acorns, and possibly eggs and small animals such as birds.

The red panda you see in the tree is sleeping. Red pandas are nocturnal and also active before sunrise and at twilight, or *crepuscular.* They are sometimes active for short periods during the day.

The red panda wakes. It makes a sound like a baby. One of the native names for the red panda is "wah," after one of the sounds that it makes. It is sometimes called "child of the mountains."

A visitor at a zoo recently stopped to look at a red panda. "It looks like a raccoon," she said, "but it has a giant panda's face."

Along with bamboo, this red panda gets his own
panda pudding every day. The pudding is made of
applesauce, banana baby food, evaporated milk,
high-protein baby cereal, vitamins, alfalfa leaves,
and dog chow. Here he is eating a treat of fruit.

What is a red panda? Is this small animal, which weighs from 7 to 14 pounds (3.2–6.4 kg), a close cousin of the giant panda, which weighs from 220 to 330 pounds (100–150 kg)? Or is it a strange-looking raccoon?

What scientific families do the red pandas and the giant pandas belong to? How closely are the two pandas related? These questions have been argued by scientists since the first scientific paper was written about the red panda in 1821 and the giant panda (known to the Chinese people as *beishung*, meaning "white bear") was discovered in 1869 by a Jesuit missionary.

The confusion about where to place these animals began with the red panda's scientific name. Though the red panda became popularly known as a panda, it was given the scientific name *Ailurus fulgens*. This means "fire-colored cat" or "shining cat."

The red panda is about the size of a cat, pads softly, and has fire-colored fur. But no scientist really considers the red panda a close relative of the cat. The red panda looks most like a raccoon.

The first scientist to study the body of a red panda was unsure of whether or not to place the red panda with the raccoon family. The red panda's teeth were similar to those of raccoons, but there were a number of other differences.

Then the giant panda was discovered. Here was another animal from Asia that ate mostly bamboo. It also had teeth similar to a raccoon's and a skull like the red panda. The giant panda's discoverer first called it a bear. But scientists could not agree. Some said it was in the raccoon family. Some said it was in the bear family. Some said that

Some scientists
think raccoons
are the red
pandas' closest
cousins, but
other scientists
think red pandas
and giant pandas
are the closest
of cousins.

In the wild, red pandas seek safety from
their enemies in the trees. Their enemies are
jackals, wild dogs, bears, leopards, and tigers.

the red panda and the giant panda should be placed together in a family of their own. This scientific argument is still going on!

All of these animals—bears, raccoons, giant pandas, and red pandas—are related. At one time they all shared a common ancestor. Scientists are not debating whether or not they are cousins but how close they are.

You have discovered the red panda in its cloud forests. Now be an explorer in another way. Listen to what the different scientists say and why. Then make up your own mind about how closely the red and giant pandas are related.

The giant panda's size and short, stubby tail make people think that it is a bear. But some scientists say that the giant panda's skeleton doesn't look like the skeleton of a real bear.

The giant panda and the red panda have similar skulls and teeth. Remember that teeth are important in deciding how closely related animals are. But some scientists say that red pandas and giant pandas have similar teeth only because they both eat bamboo. When two animals who are not closely related develop similar traits because they live in similar habitats, eat the same food, etc., this is called *convergent evolution.*

Both pandas have a "panda's thumb," which is really a small wrist bone that has developed into a thumblike structure that helps the animals grasp bamboo. This is a striking similarity, but it too could be explained by convergent evolution.

Bears and both pandas walk with their forepaws turned in. Raccoons do not walk that way.

Red and giant pandas' reproductive organs are similar.

Even with their great size difference, red pandas and giant pandas are both pregnant for about 5 months. Red pandas raise one to four cubs. Red panda cubs are born in summer, from May to July, and stay with their mother through their first winter.

Giant pandas do not growl like bears. They bleat. Red pandas make a similar sound.

But what about the red panda's long tail? The tail is similar to a raccoon's tail. But both raccoons and red pandas spend a lot of time in trees. A tail helps them balance. That long tail could be the result of convergent evolution.

If red pandas and giant pandas are close cousins, why is their coloring so different? Look closely at the red panda. Pretend that you can change all of the red to white. Now what does it look like? Some scientists think that the giant panda evolved from a smaller red-panda-type animal. They think that with its large size the giant panda no longer needed camouflage, but instead it needed a signal warning of the powerful bite it could give an enemy. The giant panda's black and white coloring makes an easily visible warning signal.

Laboratory tests also give mixed results. Studies of the blood of red pandas, giant pandas, bears, and raccoons indicate that giant pandas and bears are related and that red pandas are more closely related to both of them than to raccoons.

Another recent series of tests, including one that examined the *DNA* of these animals, places the red pandas with the raccoons and the giant pandas with the bears. DNA is an important chemical that contains the instructions that

This Styan's red panda is native to the high mountains of
northeastern Burma and southwestern China, and is larger
and a darker rusty red color than other red pandas.

determine traits, such as size and eye color, that an animal inherits from its parents. Many scientists believe that this test solved the argument.

Still, other scientists recently wrote an article in the *Journal of Mammology* which said, "Current behavioral information appears to be consistent with the interpretation that the giant panda evolved from a small, bamboo-eating animal resembling the red panda." These scientists believe that both pandas are more closely related to bears than to raccoons and that giant pandas and red pandas are the closest cousins.

Perhaps some day another scientist, perhaps you, will find new evidence.

Like the giant pandas, red pandas are also thought to be endangered in the wild because their habitat is being destroyed. Conservation areas have been established in Nepal and China, and fortunately, red pandas are easier to breed in zoos than are giant pandas. Red pandas live about 12 years in zoos. Many zoos are working together to help the red panda, the "child of the mountains," survive.

CHAPTER FOUR

TAPIR
LONG-NOSED AND
LONG-SURVIVING

South of the range of the red panda, in the rain forests of Burma, Thailand, western Malaysia, and Sumatra, you can hear the piercing whistle of an excited tapir in the night. Tapirs are usually solitary animals, but this animal is playing with its mate. You hear the other tapir clucking in reply.

The tapirs are jumping up and down. In the moonlight, you see one of the animals lifting its long, flexible nose to sniff possible danger, pricking its sensitive, white-rimmed ears toward danger. Frightened, the tapir blows air through its nose. Its sounds change into growls. Its ears point backward. Hide, because if a tapir cannot retreat into the forest or into water, it will charge. Luckily, it will not be able to see you well with its small, red-rimmed eyes.

Farther down the well-worn path that tapirs make, you will see a single calf with its mother. Unlike its parents, the baby is striped and spotted. This coloring protects the calf in the forest. Its stout body makes the calf look like a watermelon on legs.

If you could explore back in time 20 million years ago, you would see tapirs like these. A strong sense of hearing and smell have helped tapirs survive with little change for at least 20 to 30 million years.

You have been watching a Malayan tapir. Malayan tapirs are sometimes called blanket tapirs because of the white coloring across the back and rump, which looks like a white blanket covering the middle of the otherwise black animal. This coloring protects the tapir, which is mainly nocturnal, from its enemies, leopards and tigers. In the moonlit forest,

A story from Thailand tells that after the animals had been made, the Creator made one more animal out of the leftovers and called it *psom-sett,* meaning "mixture is finished." The psom-sett was the tapir.

the tapir looks like a combination of light and forest shadows.

The Malayan tapir is one of four species of tapirs. The other three tapirs—the Brazilian or South American tapir; the Mountain or Woolly tapir; and Baird's tapir—are found in wooded, grassy, and swampy areas in South America. Baird's tapir is also found in Mexico and Central America.

All of these tapirs are reddish brown with white-rimmed ears. South American and Baird's tapirs have manes.

The Woolly tapir is found high in the Andes Mountains. It is named for its thick coat, which protects it from the cold. The other tapirs have tough skin lightly covered with hair.

All tapir calves have the same watermelon camouflage. The calves' stripes and spots are gone after 6 months. Then the calves will begin to stray from their mothers. Tapirs weigh between 500 and 660 pounds (227–299 kg). The Malayan tapir is the largest of the four species. All tapirs are similar in behavior.

Can you guess who are the tapir's closest cousins? Its long nose looks like an elephant's trunk. It loves water as do hippopotamuses. It looks like a large pig. But tapirs are not closely related to any of these animals. The tapir's feet are the clue to who its cousins are.

Tapirs are a part of a group of animals called *perissodactyls*, the odd-toed ungulates. The other perissodactyls are rhinoceroses and horses. All of these animals support their weight on the third toe of each foot.

This does not mean that these modern animals all have three toes. It means that as these animals evolved, the third

Tapirs seldom vary
their routine. They use
the same route over
and over, making paths
to water. If frightened,
tapirs may escape to
water and can stay
underneath for several
minutes. Top: a Baird's
tapir (left) and South
American tapirs; bottom:
two woolly tapirs.

Right: An African black rhinoceros. This kind of rhino, along with all species of rhinoceroses, is in danger of becoming extinct. Rhinoceroses live in Africa and Southeast Asia. Bottom: A European wild horse. Horses are related to rhinoceroses and tapirs.

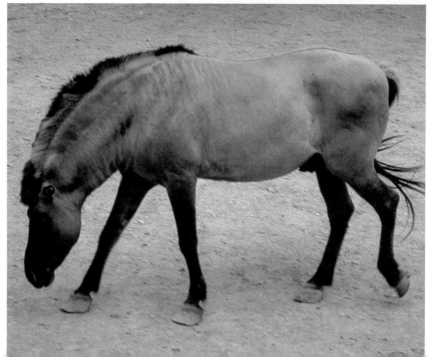

toe became the most developed. Other toes may even have disappeared. Horses now have only one toe, but that toe is the third toe. Rhinoceroses actually have three toes on each foot. Tapirs have three toes on their hind feet and four toes on their front feet.

Tapirs are more closely related to rhinoceroses than to horses. Fossils show that rhinoceroses are offshoots of an earlier tapir family. Tapirs have changed the least from their early ancestors. Horses have evolved the most.

There are several similarities between rhinos and tapirs. Both have poor eyesight but a good sense of hearing and smell. Both blow through their noses when excited. The Cincinnati Zoo's tapirs, Patrick, born on Saint Patrick's Day, and Denise, have the same personalities as rhinos. Zoo-keeper Herb Kingsbury says, "If anything new is introduced to the rhino's area, it becomes extremely alert, perks its ears up, and charges. And these tapirs will do exactly the same thing. If there is no way out, they'll just charge."

To avoid startling the tapirs and risking a charge, keepers always let tapirs know they're coming by whistling hello. Sometimes the tapirs whistle back.

The intelligence of tapirs and rhinos is also about the same. Neither rhinos nor tapirs are as smart as horses.

Tapirs in the wild eat leaves, sprouts, small branches, fruits, grasses, and aquatic plants. The tapir's long, flexible nose helps it to smell food and to grasp food otherwise out of reach. Some scientists think that the tapir's long nose helped it to survive so long by enabling it to search out food when little was available. The tapir's nose also helps it sense its enemies—leopards and tigers for the Malayan tapir, jaguars for the tapirs in Central and South America, and bears for the Woolly tapir—in time to escape.

Today, though, it is not tigers or bears that threaten the survival of tapirs. All species of tapirs except South American tapirs are endangered species. Their forest homes are being destroyed by logging. Recent research shows that tapirs may not be able to survive in forests where the original plants have been destroyed. Preserving the tapir's habitat is vital.

Zoos are also important to the tapir's survival. It is hoped that Denise and Patrick will breed. Then, in 400 days, a new tapir calf will be born, a new member of a family of animals that has existed for over 20 million years.

CHAPTER FIVE

WOMBAT
THE KOALA'S
CITY-BUILDING COUSIN

Travel back to the time of the ancient reptiles, the dinosaurs. About 90 million years ago, there was a division among another kind of animal, the mammal.

All of the animals discussed in this book are mammals. Unlike reptiles, mammals can help control their own body temperature instead of depending on outside heat or cold. In general, mammals have backbones and hair, and they nurse their young with milk. People are mammals.

Most mammals are placental mammals: They give birth to young that are fully developed. People are placental mammals. The placenta is an organ that develops during pregnancy and lets the mother pass food and oxygen to the baby growing inside her body. It takes wastes away from the baby and keeps it safe from germs. Without the placenta, the baby could not become fully developed before birth.

The other mammals that developed 90 million years ago are called *marsupials*. Marsupials do not have placentas, and their young are born very underdeveloped. A marsupial baby may be as small as a cherry at birth, and it does not even have eyes when it is born. The young marsupial climbs up and attaches itself to one of its mother's nipples, where it is fed and continues to grow. "Marsupial" comes from a word meaning pouch. Usually, but not always, the mother has a pouch in which the baby lives as it grows.

Marsupials became the main mammals of the continent of Australia because 45 million years ago Australia broke away from other lands. No placental mammals survived in

Wombats are not as slow and bumbling as they appear. Over short distances, they can run almost 25 miles (40 km) per hour.

Australia at that time. For millions of years there were no placental mammals to compete with the marsupials for food and homes.

Australian marsupials that you probably know about are kangaroos and koalas. Meet another marsupial. Meet the wombat.

Koalas are sometimes called koala bears, but they are not related to bears. Bears are placental mammals; koalas are marsupial mammals like kangaroos.

Time-travel forward to a road in modern Australia. A yellow road sign states: Wombats—Next 12 km. There is a picture of a fat animal with short legs. The wombat, who weighs 42 to 86 pounds (19–39 kg), looks like a big groundhog.

The wombat is not the groundhog's cousin. Groundhogs are placental mammals. Wombats are marsupials. The wombat is the koala's closest cousin and is a distant cousin to the kangaroo.

The wombat looks like a groundhog because it lives as a groundhog does. Both wombats and groundhogs are burrowers. Wombats are built for *burrowing*. Their thick bodies are powerful. They have short, strong legs with shovel-like claws.

Wombats can build burrows large enough for a child to crawl through. The burrows may have several entrances, side tunnels, and resting rooms. Though each wombat seems to stay to itself except to mate, the burrows often connect into an underground wombat city. One wombat city that was found was 2,625 feet by 197 feet (800 × 60 m). This is wider than one football field and about the length of seven football fields lined up in a row!

A wombat's teeth are like a groundhog's teeth. They never stop growing. They allow the wombat to eat roots and tough grasses. The grasses wear down teeth, so if the wombat's teeth didn't keep growing, it couldn't eat.

Because they reproduce their young so differently, it is easy to see that wombats and groundhogs are not close cousins. Wombats and groundhogs look and act alike because of convergent evolution.

Why is the wombat the koala's closest cousin? Michael Dulaney at the Cincinnati Zoo helped care for visiting koala

Tully and visiting wombat Wally. Michael calls wombats and koalas "the oddities of the odd marsupials." He says, "It is easier to see the differences between koalas and wombats."

Koalas spend most of their time in trees. With rare exceptions, they eat only eucalyptus leaves. Wombats spend all of their time on and in the ground. They eat grasses, roots, and other plants.

Both wombats and koalas have very short tails. Some scientists think that the tree-dwelling koala's short tail suggests that its ancestor was a ground-dwelling, wombat-like animal who didn't need a long tail for balancing in the trees.

Another hint that the koala's ancestor may have been a wombat-like animal is that a koala's pouch, which is on its belly, opens toward its hind legs instead of opening at the top as does a kangaroo's pouch. A wombat's pouch also opens at the bottom. The wombat's bottom-opening pouch keeps dirt from flying up into the pouch when the wombat is digging. A top-opening pouch would seem to make more sense for the tree-living koala.

Koalas do not need wombats' continually growing teeth, but their teeth are otherwise similar. And chemicals in the blood of koalas and wombats are also similar.

Look at the wombat's face and the koala's face. They both have small eyes and large noses. Both koalas and wombats are mainly nocturnal animals. They do not need to see as well as they need to smell and hear.

Both koalas and wombats have adapted to Australia's weather. Some people think that the word koala comes from a word of the native Aboriginal people meaning "drink not."

The word *wombat* comes from an Aboriginal word
that sounded like "wombach" to early European
settlers of Australia. One scientist suggests that the
Aboriginals may have been saying, "good to eat."

This wombat's zoo diet consists of
sweet potatoes, carrots, apples, corn on the
cob, rabbit food, monkey biscuits, and hay.

Koalas actually get much of their water from eucalyptus leaves.

Wombats can also live on little water and get water from their food, especially the hairy-nosed wombats, who live in the dry plains, grasslands, woodlands, and shrub areas of Australia. Hairy-nosed wombats have hairier muzzles, finer fur, and longer, more pointed ears than other wombats.

The common wombats, also called naked-nosed, live in eucalyptus forests along the southeast coast of Australia, as do their koala cousins. Common wombats also live in coastal grasslands and on the Australian islands of Tasmania and Flinders.

A mother wombat is pregnant for only 20 days. She gives birth to one young. The baby lives in its mother's pouch for 6 to 9 months. The young wombat may occasionally return to the pouch over the next 3 months. When about 1½ years old, the young wombat no longer needs its mother's milk.

Wombats can live for over 20 years in zoos, but it is difficult for them to breed and produce their young there. They can injure one another with their strong teeth and are difficult to keep together.

Wombats can also be hard for their keepers to get along with. They are described as making a "hissing, whistling sound" to their keepers. The wombat's sound has also been described as a hoarse, growling cough, or a warning that the animal is annoyed.

It is hard for wombats to survive. Sometimes there isn't enough rain where they live. Then their food supply is decreased, and they do not reproduce. They are killed by Australian wild dogs (dingoes). They are run over by cars. In some areas of Australia, they are killed by ranchers because they damage fences. Most of all, they are endangered because cattle, sheep, and rabbits have now been brought to Australia and compete with wombats for their habitat. One kind of wombat, the northern hairy-nosed wombat, is especially endangered. Areas such as a part of Australia's Epping Forest National Park, fenced to keep cattle out, are helping the northern hairy-nosed wombat survive.

GLOSSARY

burrow—to dig into the ground as if to make a tunnel.

canine teeth—the often pointed teeth next to the incisor teeth.

classify—to group animals (or plants), usually depending on how closely they are related. From distantly to closely related, these divisions are kingdom, phylum, class, order, family, genus, and species.

cloven—divided into two parts.

convergent evolution—the process that takes place when two animals, not closely related, develop similar traits because they live in similar habitats, eat the same food, etc.

crepuscular—active before sunrise and at twilight.

dingoes—reddish-brown wild dogs that live in Australia.

DNA—a chemical that contains the instructions for determining what traits an animal (or plant) inherits.

evolve—to develop over time from one kind of animal (or plant) to another kind.

fossils—hardened remains of plants or animals.

habitat—the place where an animal (or plant) lives.

incisor teeth—the front teeth, used for cutting.

marsupial—a mammal without a placenta, who gives birth to live, but undeveloped, young.

nocturnal—active at night.

paenungulates—a group of mammals who are related and have primitive claws more like nails than hooves.

perissodactyls—a group of hoofed mammals that support their weight on the third toe of each foot.

species—a group of individual animals (or plants) that are the same kind of animal (or plant) and can breed and produce young.

ungulate—a mammal with hooves.

FOR FURTHER READING

Burton, Maurice, and Robert Burton. *The International Wildlife Encyclopedia*, 20 vols. New York: Marshall Cavendish Corp., 1969.

Crimp, Donald J., ed. *National Geographic Book of Mammals*. 2 vols. Washington, D.C.: National Geographic Society, 1981.

Greaves, Nick. "Why the Dassie Has No Tail (a Xhosa Fable)." In *When Hippo Was Hairy and Other Tales from Africa*. New York: Barron's, 1988.

Hart, Terese B., and John A. Hart. "Tracking the Rainforest Giraffe." *Animal Kingdom* 91, January/February, (1988):26–32.

MacClintock, Dorcas. *A Natural History of Giraffes*. New York: Charles Scribner's Sons, 1973.

MacClintock, Dorcas. *Red Pandas: A Natural History*. New York: Charles Scribner's Sons, 1988.

MacDonald, David, ed. *The Encyclopedia of Mammals*. New York: Facts on File, 1984.

Patent, Dorothy Hinshaw. *Raccoons, Coatimundis, and Their Family*. New York: Holiday House, 1979.

Roberts, Miles. "The Fire Fox." *Animal Kingdom* 85, February/March, (1982):20–27.

Vandenbeld, John. *Nature of Australia: A Portrait of the Island Continent*. New York: Facts on File, 1988.

Wexo, John Bonnett. *Koalas*. Zoobooks, vol. 5, no. 9. San Diego, California: Wildlife Education, Ltd., June 1988.

INDEX

ABOUT THE AUTHOR

Geraldine Marshall Gutfreund
has a degree in zoology from
the University of Kentucky.

She writes both fiction and
nonfiction about both real
and imaginary animals.

She lives in Mount Healthy, Ohio,
near Cincinnati, with her
husband, Mark, their daughters,
Audrey and Rachel, and a
dachshund dog, Newton.
A chipmunk named Nuts lives
under their flower garden.